Ask Oliver

The Mystery of the Missing Train

Ask Oliver

The Mystery of the

Missing Train

by Terrance Dicks

Illustrated by Valerie Littlewood

Designed by Nicholas Thirkell & Partners

Printed by Garden City Press, Letchworth, Herts.
Typeset by V & M Graphics Ltd, Aylesbury Bucks

For Piccadilly Press, 1984
64 Greenfield Gardens, London NW2 1HY

ISBN 0 946826 03 X

Chapter One

On Safari

Oliver looked at the lion - and the lion looked straight back at Oliver.

It padded slowly towards him, muscles rippling under a tawny coat. Its jaws opened wide, revealing great yellow teeth.

The lion yawned, strolled slowly past the car, disappeared into the trees on the other side of the road.

The gang - Oliver, Pete, Vicky and Gupta - gave huge sighs of relief. However many times you've been to a Safari Park, seeing a real live lion a few feet away is a bit of a shock.

'Blow,' said Pete. 'I should have got a picture.' Pete had brought his new camera.

Oliver's father started the car and they drove on their way.

It was the first Saturday of the Easter holidays. They were celebrating with a trip to the local Safari Park, which had just re-opened after the winter close-down.

The Safari Park was shaped like a cart-wheel, a big circle with a smaller circle inside.

The small circle held the cafe, gift shop and toilets as well as the big old house where Lord Buckleigh lived. Lord Buckleigh was quite a famous explorer. He had set up the Safari Park in the grounds of his Stately Home.

Oliver's father parked the car and they piled into the cafe for crisps and coke.

'Right, where do we go first?' he asked.

'Let's go back and see the monkeys,' said Pete. He was a tall red-headed boy, the leader of the gang. He was very fond of the monkeys. Perhaps it was because, like him, they were always getting into mischief.

Victoria, Vicky for short, wanted to go to the Zoo Park and see the deer and the wallabies. She was a gentle, serious girl, and she liked gentle serious animals.

'I should like to feed the dolphins,' announced Gupta, a round-faced cheerful boy with a fund of terrible jokes. Gupta liked dolphins because they were always jolly, their little round eyes twinkling with some secret joke.

Everyone looked at Oliver.

Oliver was the youngest and smallest of Pete's gang. He didn't talk much, but what he said was always sensible. He was good at solving problems. Like Vicky, Oliver wanted to go to the Zoo - they had a new attraction, a cave with real vampire bats - but he knew that suggesting this would just keep the argument going. They needed a compromise. 'Why don't we have a ride on the train? That way we'll get a quick look at everything. Then we can work our way round, section by section.'

*   *   *

The steam train was one of the Safari Park's main attractions. It ran from the main station at the centre out to the edge of the Park. It went right round the Park, passing through all the different sections, stopping at a little station in each one, and then back to the centre again.

The best thing was that the train ride was included in the

entry price, and you could go round as many times as you liked.

Everyone agreed to Oliver's plan.

Pete found this a bit annoying. *He* was supposed to be the boss of the gang, yet they always seemed to end up doing what Oliver said. The trouble was, Oliver's plans were always so fair and sensible. It was hard to think of anything against them!

Leaving Oliver's father in the cafe, they went to the station and joined the little crowd waiting for the train. The station had an old-fashioned look, with a wooden fence and platform and tin signs advertising traditional products like Bovril and Virol, and Lipton's Teas.

They heard the distant 'whoo -

whoo' of the train whistle, and everyone stared down the long straight section of track which led to the outer ring of track that ran round the Safari Park.

There was a low hill with a tunnel through it at the end of the track, and a little wood on the other side.

They could see the smoke from the engine rising above the trees. They heard the *chuff, chuff, chuff,* of the engine, the *whoo-whoo* of the whistle as the train chugged out of the wood and into the tunnel.

The engine noise faded for a moment then the little train steamed triumphantly out of the tunnel, a splendid old-fashioned little steam engine pulling three open coaches. With much clanking and hissing of steam, it pulled into the station. The passengers got off and the four friends climbed on board, making for the carriage just behind the engine.

There was the usual wait while the engine driver stoked up the boiler with bundles of wood from the huge pile beside the track. There was a brass name-plate on the boiler - *The African Belle*.

Suddenly they heard loud, angry voices coming from just outside the station.

They turned and saw a little group, gathered around a big black car which was parked by the station entrance. There was a burly red-faced man in tweeds, a thin-faced man in a dark suit, and a uniformed chauffeur.

The burly, red-faced man was shouting, 'For the last time, will you stop pestering me! I'm telling you just as I told your precious boss. You tell your Mr. James that this engine's not for sale, and never will be - especially not to him!'

The thin-faced man said something in reply, speaking in a low angry voice.

'Right!' roared the big man. 'That's it! Get off my property,

and don't come back!' (He pro-
nounced 'off' as if it was spelt
'orf'.) He grabbed the other man
and literally threw him into the
back of the waiting car. The
chauffeur got the door open just
in time.

Closing the door, the terrified
chauffeur ran hurriedly round to
the front of the car, jumped in and
drove away at top speed.

The big man strode off.

'What was all that about?' asked
Pete.

'That was Lord Buckleigh, the
owner of this place.' said Oliver.
'His picture's in the guide we
bought.'

(Oliver always read programmes
and guides very carefully all the
way through. He said people

often missed vital information when it was right under their noses.)

Vicky said, 'Well, it's pretty obvious what was happening. The other man wanted to buy this engine, and Lord Buckleigh isn't selling.'

Gupta's eyes opened wide. 'Who would want to be buying a racketty old engine like this?'

'I'll have you know young man this steam engine's unique,' said a

fussy voice behind them. 'It's the only one of its kind in the world.'

They turned and saw a bald-headed, bespectacled little man in a shabby blue suit, sitting at the back of the carriage.

'Are you keen on steam engines then?' asked Oliver politely.

'I suppose I'm a fanatic really. This particular engine was designed and built by Lord Buckleigh's grandfather for use on his plantation in Africa. It's been in the family for years and it's in perfect condition. You see the unusually large fire-box? That's because it's specially adapted for wood burning . . .'

He went on telling them about the engine for quite some time.

The four children listened politely, but they were quite glad when the whistle of the engine announced that they were about to set off.

They jolted along the track to the edge of the Safari Park, holding on tight as the train plunged into the darkness of the tunnel. Im-

Immediately the smell of steam filled the air. An alarming stream of sparks from the wood burning engine glowed like fireworks in the darkness of the tunnel.

The train puffed its way around the Safari Park and the gang sat back, grinning at each other enjoying the ride.

It was their last ride before *The African Belle* disappeared.

Chapter Two

The Impossible Crime

The four friends had a lovely time at the Safari Park.

After their ride they re-joined Oliver's father and went round the different sections, one by one. Pete took a picture of practically everything.

Several hours later, Pete persuaded Oliver's father to drive them back into the Jungle Park. This didn't work out too well, because a gang of mischievous monkeys ambushed the car, climbing all over it.

Oliver's father was far from pleased when the biggest and boldest monkey tried to eat one of his wing-mirrors. He frightened the monkey off with a loud toot on the horn, and drove angrily away.

'It could be worse,' said Gupta. 'An elephant could have sat on us.'

Oliver's father didn't laugh.

When they got back to the centre area, he found big tooth marks in the rubber around the mirror's edge.

Oliver's father stood examining the marks, muttering to himself. He took a great pride in his car.

'We'll just pop off to the train,' said Oliver hastily. 'We should be in time for the last ride of the day.'

But they weren't.

When they reached the station, the train was just pulling away.

Pete checked the time on his

new digital watch. 'It's leaving four minutes early!'

Vicky looked sadly after the train. 'We should have got here early too!'

'Maybe the train was full up and they just decided to go,' said Oliver.

A woman nearby overheard him. She was holding the hands of

two sobbing children. 'It was full up all right. This gang of young men pushed their way to the front of the queue and filled up the whole train. As soon as they were on board, the engine driver jumped on and drove away. I called out to ask if there'd be another ride, and he just laughed and yelled, 'Don't count on it, lady!'

'Curioser and curioser,' said Oliver.

The woman led her children away.

Oliver, Vicky, Pete and Gupta stood on the platform, watching the train steam away down the track. Pete took a picture of it.

'Well, there she goes,' said a familiar voice. They turned and saw the little man with glasses, the train fanatic who'd lectured them earlier. Presumably he'd missed his ride too, though he seemed oddly cheerful about it. He nodded to the children and drifted away.

They heard another, familiar voice. 'What's going on? Is there something wrong?' It was Lord Buckleigh. He'd just seen the angry mother marching off.

Oliver explained what had happened.

Lord Buckleigh frowned. 'That's very odd! Can't understand it. Tell you what, you hang on here, and when the train gets back I'll tell him to make one more trip, just for you.'

'That's very kind of you,' said Vicky.

'Quite all right, my dear. Can't have dissatisfied customers, can we? She'll be back in about ten minutes.'

'More like twenty,' thought Oliver, though he was too polite to say so.

It took the little train almost twenty-five minutes to make the round trip – Oliver had timed it.

The train had reached the end of the straight stretch of track by now and was entering the tunnel. They heard it toot as it vanished into the darkness.

Lord Buckleigh frowned. 'She's moving much too fast!'

'Maybe the driver's in a hurry to get home,' suggested Pete.

They all stood staring towards the wood. It was dusk now, and

they couldn't see the train, but
they could hear the whistle, and
see the engine smoke rising above
the trees, as the train came out of
the tunnel.

There was a final triumphant
'Whooo-whooo-whooo!' from the
whistle. The train noises faded
away into silence.

'Overdoing the whistle a bit,'

grumbled Lord Buckleigh. 'And she's definitely moving too fast. Don't know what's got into young Fred!' He looked at his watch. 'Still, shouldn't be long now. The rate he's going that engine'll be back here in no time.'

But it wasn't.

*   *   *

They waited ten minutes, fifteen and then twenty, with Lord Buckleigh growing more and more impatient.

After twenty-five minutes he said, 'We should be able to hear her coming back by now.' They all listened, but there wasn't a chuff or toot-toot. Lord Buckleigh looked at the four children. 'Sorry, but we'll have to forget the extra ride. Fred must have a breakdown somewhere along the line.

'Listen,' said Oliver suddenly.

Everyone listened.

'Still can't hear her,' said Lord Buckleigh.

'No, not the train,' said Oliver. 'Something else. A sort of thumping sound. It's coming from the engine shed.'

'So it is!' Lord Buckleigh led the way into the shed - and bent over a bound figure kicking its legs

furiously against the wall. 'It's young Fred!'

They untied the engine driver and helped him to his feet. 'It was all those blokes,' he gasped. 'Bundled me in here, took my overalls and my cap.'

'And went for a joy-ride on my train!' said Lord Buckleigh grimly.

'Wait till I get my hands on them!'

He dashed off towards the wood, bounding along at tremendous speed, like an angry lion hunting its prey.

'Come on,' said Oliver, and set off down the track.

The others followed.

They reached the end of the tunnel just in time to see Lord

Buckleigh disappearing over the hill top. Clearly he hadn't bothered with the tunnel at all.

Oliver and the others moved up to the tunnel mouth, and moved cautiously inside.

It was gloomy in the tunnel, but there was enough light to see the dark shapes of the railway carriages.

'That's impossible,' gasped Vicky. 'We *saw* the train leave, and it's still here!'

Oliver went further along the tunnel. 'The carriages are here but the engine isn't!'

The three open passenger-carriages stood a little way inside the tunnel - but the engine had gone.

Gupta said, 'They have uncoupled the engine and driven it away by itself.'

Oliver looked inside the carriages, one by one. There was something bundled up on the seat in the front one. 'It's the driver's overalls!' Oliver felt something hard in the pocket. Reaching inside he fished the something out - it was a big bundle of pound notes, held together with a rubber band. 'I'd better just leave it all here – mustn't disturb the evidence'!

More puzzled than ever the gang moved along the tunnel, heading for the circle of light at the far end.

They emerged blinking into daylight – and found themselves looking at a lion.

It might have been the very same lion they had seen in the Jungle Park.

This time there was no car to protect them.

The lion began stalking towards them.

Chapter Three

The Quickness of the Hand . . .

Pete remembered his position – fearless leader of the gang. 'Nobody move. Don't scream or shout, and whatever you do, don't run!'

Pete moved very slowly to the front of the group.

He stared at the lion very hard.

Wasn't there supposed to be something about the mystic powers of the human eye.

The lion stared back. It padded right up to Pete and licked his arm, with a great rough tongue like a cat's.

Pete stood very very still.

He wasn't sure if the lion was

being friendly, or seeing what he tasted like.

A voice shouted, 'Goldy! Come here at once!'

Pete looked up and saw Lord Buckleigh hurrying towards him, followed by a keeper with a harness and a leash.

Lord Buckleigh fished in his pocket, took something out, unwrapped it and held it out. 'Here Goldy.'

The lion turned and ambled over, licking the sweet from his hand.

'Toffee,' explained Lord Buckleigh. 'Goldy loves toffees. Bad for him really but in an emergency . . . Well done, young man, you did exactly the right thing.'

Goldy was still chewing contentedly as the keeper put him on the leash and led him away.

'How did the lion get out?' asked Pete, trying to stop his knees wobbling.

'Someone opened a section of fence between this section and the Jungle Park, and drove some kind of vehicle through. We're repairing the gap now.'

'Have you found the engine?' asked Oliver.

'Not a trace! I've searched right through the woods and beyond, and I've got keepers searching the whole Safari Park.'

Oliver said, 'We searched the tunnel. The carriages are there, but not the engine. We found the driver's overalls with some money in.'

Lord Buckleigh stared at him in astonishment.

Oliver's father came running up, 'What's going on? Why are you all over here? Where's the train?'

'Someone's stolen it!'

While Lord Buckleigh told

Oliver's father what had happened the gang *was* trying to work out *how* it had happened.

'Helicopters!' said Pete. 'One of those giant troop-carrying helicopters they've got in America. They could drop down steel cables with hooks on the end . . .'

Gupta gave him a pitying look. 'You don't think that someone would be noticing a helicopter flying along with a steam engine dangling from it?'

'Like us, for instance,' suggested Vicky.

Oliver said nothing. As usual, he was thinking hard.

Lord Buckleigh said, 'I've telephoned the police and they're on their way. I'm afraid I'll have to ask you all to stay till they get here.'

'Why us? You don't think *we* stole your engine, do you?' Oliver's father held out his arms. 'I'm quite willing to be searched!'

'No, of course not! But I need these children as witnesses. When I called the police station they obviously thought I was raving mad!'

Suddenly, they heard a weird electronic howling noise. A white police car was whizzing along the nearby road towards them, blue light flashing on the top, with a big blue police van close behind it.

*   *   *

After that it was, as Oliver's father said later, a proper circus. There were keen young policemen everywhere, and what seemed like a whole pack of police dogs as well.

It was getting dark now but the police had brought big torches and portable searchlights. They

studied every inch of the tunnel and the track for clues, without success. Then they swarmed all over the Safari Park.

For a while Fred came under suspicion because of the money in his overalls. But as he said, if he had been bribed to help the robbers, he'd have hidden the money a bit more carefully.

Lord Buckleigh said he'd known Fred for years, and he was sure he was honest.

The police inspector, a worried looking man with grey hair, had questioned all four children over and over again.

'You saw the train go down the track, and into the tunnel?'

'Yes,' said Gupta. 'I am seeing it with my own eyes.'

'And you're sure it came out of the tunnel and into the woods?'

'Yes,' said Vicky. 'Quite sure. We saw it go!'

Oliver said, 'We heard the whistle and saw the smoke from the funnel.'

'And that's the last you or anyone saw of it?'

'Yes,' said Oliver patiently. 'The

carriages stayed in the tunnel but the engine didn't.'

Several hours later, the inspector sighed. 'I'm sorry, Lord Buckleigh, but we've done all we can tonight. We've searched the entire Safari Park, and we haven't found a thing. I'll be back tomorrow with more men and we'll broadcast, make an appeal for witnesses. Meanwhile, as they say in detective stories, the police are baffled. We need Sherlock Holmes.'

Gupta said, 'We are not needing Sherlock Homes. We have our Oliver.'

But for the moment, Oliver was baffled too.

*   *   *

'Another piece of cake,' suggested Lord Buckleigh. 'Some more coke?'

Pete shook his head. 'No thank you. I can hardly move as it is!'

They were in the big old-fashioned kitchen of Lord Buckleigh's house. He had been very apologetic about holding them up. Since they'd all missed their suppers, he had insisted on giving them a meal.

His housekeeper had provided what Lord Buckleigh called 'a bit of a spread'. Ham and cheese and pickles and salad and a giant pork pie, with fruit cake to follow and a huge pot of tea.

Oliver's father was discussing the mystery with Lord Buckleigh.

'What beats me is, who'd want

to steal a steam engine anyway?'

'That engine's unique,' said Lord Buckleigh indignantly. 'Priceless! Collectors all over the world have been after it for years. Only today a millionaire, a fellow called Caleb James sent his agent to see me. The fellow good as asked me to name my own price. Kept on pestering me, wouldn't take no for an answer. Had to chuck him out eventually!'

Pete said, 'I know, we saw you!'

'That chap James has been after it for years. Never met him, but he gets my goat. Keeps writing to me about it. I wrote him a real stinker of a reply just recently. Told him to forget the whole thing, he'd never get his hands on *The African Belle*. Mind you, he's not the only one. I've had offers from all over the world.'

'No shortage of suspects then?'

'Hundreds,' said Lord Buckleigh gloomily. 'Thousands!'

'It's not so much the *who* that matters,' said Oliver. 'It's the *how*?'

Gupta nodded. 'This is not a Whodunnit, it is a Howdunnit!'

'It's crazy,' said Pete. 'How *can* a massive great steam engine go up in smoke?'

'It is like magic,' whispered Gupta.

'Or a very good conjuring trick,' said Vicky more practically.

'Conjuring trick?' scoffed Pete. 'You can't do conjuring tricks with steam engines!'

Oliver jumped up. 'Yes, you

can,' he shouted. 'Smoke, conjuring tricks, magic! Misdirection.
I think I've got it! The quickness
of the hand deceives the eye!'

Lord Buckleigh stared at him.
'What's the matter with you, boy?'

'I know where your steam engine is,' said Oliver simply. 'And I
can help you to catch the people
who stole it.'

'Catch them - how? They'll be
miles away by now.'

'Oh, no they won't. They'll be coming back here, tonight.'

'Whatever for?'

'To collect *The African Belle*!'

*   *   *

It was dark and spooky on the hill just beside the tunnel entrance. It was crowded too, what with Lord Buckleigh, Oliver's father, Oliver, Pete, Vicky and Gupta, and quite a lot of policemen.

A lion roared somewhere in the distance.

It had taken quite a bit of persuasion to get everyone there. Oliver was desperately hoping his theory was correct. Lord Buckleigh had been hard to convince, and so had the police when he finally agreed to phone them up.

But as Oliver's father had pointed out, it wasn't just the best theory they'd got it was the only theory they'd got.

Finally the Inspector had decided Oliver's plan was at least worth a try. He came back with all the men he could raise.

Laying flat in the darkness they waited - and waited and waited.

Oliver was beginning to despair when at last he heard the sound he had been expecting. A low, growling, roaring sound.

It was the sound of a very large vehicle being driven very, very slowly.

He jabbed the Inspector in the ribs. 'Look!'

A massive black shape was moving through the darkness towards them. A giant container lorry with lots of enormous wheels, crept through the night like a dinosaur. The lorry stopped, close to the tunnel entrance.

Can you solve the mystery? Clues: 1. Think about a steam engine and smoke.

2. The police searched the woods, but there was one place they didn't search.

Chapter Four

Oliver's Answers

Men got out, dozens of them, dressed in dark clothing, carrying tools and equipment.

The men poured into the tunnel.

Moments later there came a low clanking sound.

'The carriages,' whispered Lord Buckleigh. 'They must be pushing the empty carriages out of the other end.'

Lights sprang on inside the tunnel.

The observers rose and crept forward.

The inside of the tunnel was brightly lit up with portable

electric lamps. The rails had been lifted, the men seemed to be brushing the earth away from the tunnel floor. One man, smaller than the rest stood a little apart, 'Hurry,' he snapped. 'Quickly now.'

The earth was scraped aside, revealing wooden planking.

Working quickly and silently, the men lifted away the planks.

Beneath them was a deep pit with sloping ends. There, in the centre of the pit, gleamed *The African Belle*.

Oliver nodded to Pete, who framed the scene carefully in his camera viewfinder and pressed the button.

At the sight of the flash, everyone swung round. The little man

stepped angrily forward.

'Quite still please everyone,' shouted the inspector. 'This whole area is surrounded!'

The little man came towards them. They saw that it was the bald, bespectacled train fanatic they'd met earlier in the day - the one who'd known so much about *The African Belle.*

'Good evening, Mr. James,' said Oliver politely. 'Can we have our engine back, please?'

*   *   *

'You *all* helped me work it out,' said Oliver.

They were in Lord Buckleigh's kitchen again - it was very late now - having a final snack of cocoa and ham sandwiches before going home.

Mr. James and all his men had been carted off, and were now down at the local police station, 'helping the police with their enquiries.'

The police had gone too, all except the grey-haired Inspector.

'*How* did we help,' demanded Pete a little sulkily. As usual he felt Oliver was getting all the publicity. (Still, he thought, *he'd* been the one who'd defied the lion!)

Oliver took another swig of his cocoa. 'Well, *you* talked about the engine 'going up in smoke!'. Gupta said it was 'like magic' and Vicky said it was a 'conjuring trick'. Suddenly it all came together in my head. We were supposed to think the engine vanished by magic, but really it *was* just a conjuring trick - and the smoke was a very important part of it!'

The Inspector sighed. 'All right,

young fellow, you'd better recon-
struct the crime for us. Though
how this is all going to sound in
my report . . .'

Oliver looked round the circle
of faces and felt suddenly shy. His
father put a hand on his shoulder.
'Come on, old son, just start at the
beginning.'

'Well, I think it all started when
Mr. Caleb James kept trying to
buy *The African Belle*, and Lord
Buckleigh here wrote him a letter
- a pretty rude letter I imagine.'

Lord Buckleigh looked guilty.
'I only told him he was a jumped
up, conceited little twerp and his
money couldn't buy everything.
Oh, and I said I'd break the *Belle*
up for scrap before I'd let him
have her.'

Oliver nodded. 'I thought it was something like that. Well, Mr. James is a very rich and powerful man and he isn't used to being told off like that. So he decided to get his revenge by stealing *The African Belle* - and more important, stealing it in a way that would make Lord Buckleigh look silly.' 'That is explaining the who and the why,' said Gupta. 'How about the how?'

'That's right,' said Vicky. We all *saw* the engine come out of the tunnel and go into the wood.'

'Oh no we didn't! We saw *smoke*! We heard the engine noise and the whistle, so naturally we thought it was the train.'

Pete said, 'I get it - they faked it all!'

Oliver nodded, 'They must have broken in the night before and got everything ready. A big gang of men could do it, working all night. Then they all came back here this afternoon, crowded everybody off the last ride, got rid of the driver and drove the train to the tunnel. They sent the fake engine out of the tunnel, uncoupled the real engine and put it in the pit, covered the pit up, replaced the rails and pushed the carriages back. They had nearly half an hour, remember. When we realised the engine had disappeared you all searched the wood and the area around. Nobody looked in the tunnel, and nobody looked under the tracks. They waited till the first search died down and came back here tonight to take the engine away. They didn't dare leave it hidden too long.'

A beaming Lord Buckleigh said, 'Well, I can tell you this. You're all getting a free pass to my Safari Park for life. And if anyone steals my elephant herd or my pride of lions - I shall come and ask Oliver to get them back!'